D0492823

For Mum and Dad

Bloomsbury Publishing, London, Oxford, New Delhi, New York and Sydney

First published in Great Britain in 2015 by Bloomsbury Publishing Plc
50 Bedford Square, London, WC1B 3DP

Text and illustrations © Suzanne Barton 2015
The moral right of the author/illustrator has been asserted

All rights reserved
No part of this publication may be reproduced or
transmitted by any means, electronic, mechanical, photocopying
or otherwise, without prior permission of the publisher

A CIP catalogue record of this book is available from the British Library

ISBN 978 1 4088 5914 8

Printed in China by C & C Offset Printing Co Ltd, Shenzhen, Guandong

1 3 5 7 9 10 8 6 4 2

All papers used by Bloomsbury Publishing are natural, recyclable products made
from wood grown in well-managed forests. The manufacturing processes conform
to the environmental regulations of the country of origin

www.bloomsbury.com

BLOOMSBURY is a registered trademark of Bloomsbury Publishing Plc

Robin's Winter Song

Suzanne Barton

BLOOMSBURY
LONDON OXFORD NEW DELHI NEW YORK SYDNEY

It was a beautiful autumn day.
Robin sang from his branch as it swayed in the breeze.

He saw the leaves swirling in the wind,
twisting and turning, rising and falling.

Something was different – but what was it?

The squirrels were scurrying, the mice were scampering and, high up in the branches, the finches were fluttering.

"Are you going somewhere?"
Robin asked the finches.

"We're getting ready to fly south," they chirped.
"Winter is coming."

"Who is Winter?" asked Robin.
"And why don't you want to meet him?"

But the finches didn't hear him
and, in a flurry, they were gone.

Down on the ground, Squirrel was busy digging.

"What are you doing?" Robin asked.

"I'm burying these nuts before Winter comes," said Squirrel.

Winter sounds very greedy, thought Robin, and he flew off to the big oak tree.

"I don't like the sound of Winter at all," Robin told Owl.
"Do you think I should fly south like the finches?"

"Oh, no," said Owl. "It's too far for you.
You must stay here, but be sure to
keep warm and snug or you'll
be cold when Winter comes."

Winter is scary, greedy and cold?
Robin was frightened.

He looked on sadly as the rest of his friends flew
south – far, far away from Winter. How he
wished he could go with them.

"I hope they come back
soon," he sighed.

Later in the woods, Robin spotted Bear.
He glided down, happy to meet a friend.

"Where are you going?"
he asked.

"I'm off to find a cosy cave to sleep in
until Winter is gone," said Bear.

Even Bear was hiding! Robin remembered what
Owl had told him . . . He needed to find somewhere
warm and snug – somewhere far away from Winter.

"Can I come with you?" he asked Bear.

Robin and Bear settled comfortably
in Bear's cave.

"How many sleeps until Winter
goes away?" asked Robin.

"Just one," said Bear.

That's not so bad,
thought Robin.

He snuggled close to Bear
and squeezed his eyes shut.

Before long he heard Bear's snores, soft and gentle,
and soon Robin fell fast asleep, too.

When Robin stirred he felt a chill in the air. It was very cold. *Perhaps Winter's here*, he thought.

Robin flew to the opening of the cave and, as he peeped out, he gasped.

The whole wood had turned white.
Everything sparkled and shimmered, and
white flakes were falling from the sky.

How beautiful! thought Robin as he
tiptoed out into the fresh, crunchy white.

As Robin hopped and slipped
     happily through the wood, he came
     across all sorts of animals.

"Why is everything so white?" he asked Mouse.

"It's snow, of course," squeaked Mouse.
"Look around you, Robin. It's Winter."

"This is Winter?" gasped Robin.

He couldn't believe it. Winter wasn't scary at all.
In fact, it was wonderful!

The forest was transformed and Robin loved
exploring it with his new friends.

He chased snowflakes with Owl.

He helped Squirrel
find his acorns.

And, at night, everyone snuggled together to keep warm.

Robin was having such wonderful wintery fun that time passed quickly and, one day, he noticed shoots sprouting out of the ground. Something was different – but what was it?

Then he realised.
"The snow is melting," he said.

"That means it's time to wake Bear," said Squirrel.

Bear yawned, stretched and rubbed his eyes.
"Winter's almost gone," he sighed, happily.

"But I love Winter," said Robin, sadly.
"Why does it have to go?"

"Because Spring is coming," smiled Bear.

Robin didn't know what Spring was
but, this time, he was sure that he
wanted to find out.

"I can't wait to meet Spring!"
he sang, joyfully.